THE BUSY BEES

Ann Taylor

The Busy Bees

Once upon a time, in a beautiful garden filled with colorful flowers, there lived a group of busy bees.

They worked hard every day
to collect nectar from the
flowers and turn it into sweet,
delicious honey.

One day, a little bee named Bella decided to explore the garden on her own.

She flew from flower to flower,
taking in all the beautiful
colors and fragrances.

As she was flying, she noticed a big, black bug buzzing around her.

Bella was scared, but the bug said, "Don't be afraid, little bee.

I am a friendly bumblebee,
and I am here to help you."

Bella was curious, so she asked, "How can you help me?"

The bumblebee replied, "I can show you how to collect more nectar and pollen from the flowers.

You see, bees like us are
important pollinators, and
we help the flowers grow
and produce fruit.

Without us, the garden wouldn't be as beautiful and the animals wouldn't have food to eat."

Bella was amazed by what the bumblebee had said.

She decided to follow him and learn more about how to collect nectar and pollen.

The bumblebee taught her
how to land on a flower,

use her long tongue to suck
the nectar,

and collect pollen on her fuzzy legs.

Bella was grateful for the
bumblebee's help.

She flew back to her hive and told her friends about her adventure.

They were all excited to learn
what she had discovered and
went out to the garden to
practice what they had learned.

From that day on, the busy bees worked even harder to collect nectar and pollen from the flowers.

They flew from one flower to the next, spreading pollen and helping the garden grow.

And that's how Bella and her friends became the best pollinators in the garden,

always busy and working hard to make the world a more beautiful and tasty place.

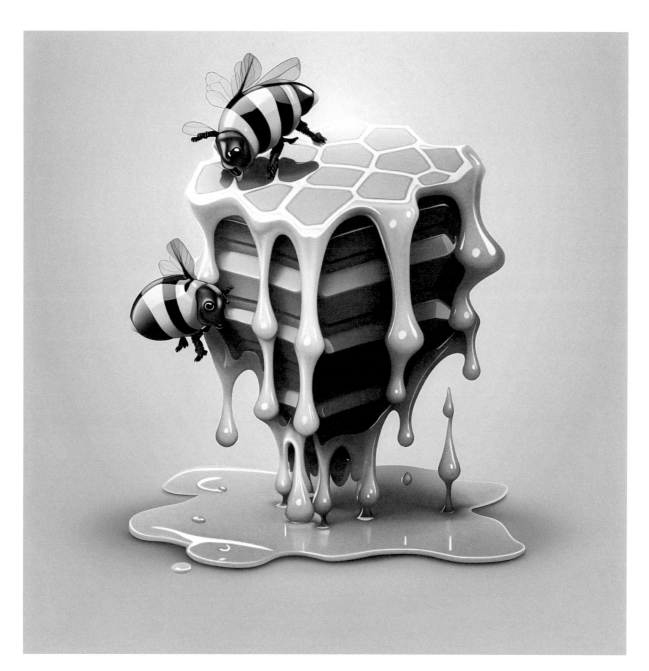

The end.

I hope you enjoyed reading this book as much as I enjoyed creating it. To find out more about me and my collection, please visit https://www.amazon.com/author/ann-taylor or scan the following QR code.

I value your support and appreciate the interest you have in my books. Your enthusiasm and feedback inspire me to keep writing, to keep creating, and to keep dreaming. So, from the bottom of my heart, thank you.

Sincerely,

Ann Taylor

Made in the USA
Thornton, CO
03/03/24 20:20:51

0d6bf357-7ac3-464e-8d18-deeda7dcc5ffR01